Not every Princess

Published by
MAGINATION PRESS
An Educational Publishing Foundation Book
American Psychological Association
750 First Street, NE
Washington, DC 20002

For more information about our books, including a complete catalog, please write to us,
call 1-800-374-2721, or visit our website at www.apa.org/pubs/magination.

Printed by Worzalla, Stevens Point, WI

Book design by Sandra Kimbell

Library of Congress Cataloging-in-Publication Data
Bone, Jeffrey.
 Not every princess / by Jeffrey Bone, PsyD, and Lisa Bone, PhD ; illustrated by Valeria Docampo.
    pages cm
 "American Psychological Association."
 "An Educational Publishing Foundation Book."
 Summary: After listing activities that are stereotypically, but not always, attributed to princesses, fairies, pirates, superheroes,
and more, encourages the reader to imagine what one could be, despite others' expectations. Includes note to parents.
 ISBN 978-1-4338-1647-5 (hardcover) — ISBN 1-4338-1647-4 (hardcover) — ISBN 978-1-4338-1648-2 (pbk.) — ISBN
1-4338-1648-2 (pbk.) [1. Stereotypes (Social psychology)—Fiction. 2. Sex role—Fiction. 3. Individuality—Fiction. 4.
Imagination—Fiction.] I. Bone, Lisa. II. Docampo, Valeria, 1976– illustrator. III. Title.
 PZ7.B636972Not 2013
 [E]—dc23
                        2013020806

Manufactured in the United States of America
First printing October 2013
10 9 8 7 6 5 4 3 2 1

Not every Princess

by Jeffrey Bone, PsyD, and Lisa Bone, PhD
illustrated by Valeria Docampo

Magination Press • Washington, DC
American Psychological Association

Not every princess
lives in a castle.

Not every fairy
has wings.

Not every pirate sails ships.

And not every bird sings.

Not all ballerinas leap
Across the stage with ease,
Acting like monkeys
And swinging by trapeze.

Not all superheroes fly.
Some don't even soar—
At least not any more
Than a kitten can roar.

Not all mermaids swim.
Some may even float,
Surfing the ocean waves
Or traveling by boat.

Not all knights fight dragons.
Some seek friends instead,
Singing them lullabies
And tucking them in bed.

But that doesn't mean
You don't have a kingdom to rule.
Just open your mind
And you'll find every tool...

To be strong

Or smart

Or brave

Or sweet.

Your imagination,
Your thoughts,
Create pictures
and scenes.

Beautiful, amazing,
picturesque dreams.

So give it a try:
Start by closing your eyes.

The rest is up to you.
Let it be a surprise.

Note to Parents and Caregivers

In 2012, a woman refereed an NFL game for the first time ever. While hopefully more and more women follow in her footsteps, her accomplishment placed a spotlight on our culture's continued enforcement of gender roles. Where did this desire to referee football come from? Why did she believe she could be the first? Is it reasonable to believe she imagined herself as a referee? There was no one to follow, no mold or model to copy. She had to create an opportunity that only existed in her imagination and challenge societal expectations and attitudes regarding gender roles.

A gender role is a set of learned behaviors and attitudes based on expectations from parents, peers, teachers, and information consumed from media such as books, games, and television. Gender roles vary among cultures and change over time. Gender role is defined through dress, grooming, play, family structure, challenges, and purpose.

Although our society has made many advances over the years regarding gender role expectations, differences in these roles and expectations continue to persist. For example, there is a stereotype that men and boys are more academically proficient in the areas of science, technology, mathematics, and engineering. Studies have demonstrated the stereotypes associated with gender roles have a significant impact on how children assess their proficiency in these academic subjects, thus limiting women's and girls' interest and participation in these fields. Stereotypes such as these can significantly impact the course of a child's life.

Additionally, children who do not adopt traditional gender roles are often targets of bullying. For example, a boy who likes to play dress-up with a tiara and boa or a girl who wants to play on the football team could be teased or ostracized for such behavior. By challenging the rigidity of gender roles, we also promote the end of bullying of those children who do not follow stereotypical gender expectations.

How This Book Can Help

Not Every Princess takes readers on a poetic journey gently questioning the rigid construction of gender roles and inspiring readers to access their imaginations and challenge societal expectations. It intends to encourage all of those princesses and pirates who did not fall into a life of castles and boats that they too are no less than what they dream to be. What makes a pirate or princess? Most kids' homes are short a moat and a drawbridge, but those princesses and pirates can nonetheless be just as regal or adventurous as they imagine, even when their thrones and pirate ships are an assortment of couch pillows.

The purpose of this book is to help children envision lives for themselves beyond stereotypical gender roles and expectations. Although your children are not settling on career paths before even starting preschool, encourage them as early as possible to listen to their own thoughts and feelings—and not to rely on mass media—for their idea of who they are and what they can achieve. Additionally, teach your children to respect the paths that others create for themselves and promote increased tolerance for children who do not follow traditional gender roles. Let your children know that judging or bullying others only limits the diversity found in our schools, workplaces, and neighborhoods.

How You Can Help

There are steps you can take to encourage your children to challenge stereotypes and gender roles, and grow into the person of their choosing.

Reveal endless possibilities. Try to expose your child to media containing men and women occupying a variety of different roles—especially those roles that are contrary to stereotypes, such as male librarians or female engineers. With such subtle exposure, you are giving permission for your child to dive into his imagination and be who he is, not who others wish he would be. This is not to say that the traditional model of mommy at home and daddy at work is a negative example. Instead, the intent is to provide children with all available possibilities of what one can be. When your child is playing with toys or engaging in imaginative play, try not to place limits due to gender. For example, boys can love the color pink or playing with dolls, while girls may enjoy playing the roles of monster, doctor, firefighter, and superhero.

Encourage imagination. If reality does not provide a figure for inspiration, a child seeking a life that has not already been written for her may turn to her imagination. An excellent way to strengthen the imagination is through reading. Reading stories with your child provides opportunities to learn of faraway lands, both real and fantastical, and helps her develop a sense of a story, scenarios, conflicts, and characters. The more she is exposed to these basic building blocks of imagination, the more comfortable she will be branching out on her own to create stories for herself. Kids are natural story tellers. You can provide the *how, who,* and *what* questions to drive their imaginations along, which may lead to the creation of new worlds and characters.

Open your mind. It is not uncommon for your daughter to want to play Superman (perhaps with you playing the helpless citizens needing to be rescued!). While your first instinct might be to tell her there is also a Super*woman,* why not let her play the role that is unfolding in her mind? If she hears that she cannot be Superman, what else would she shy away from being, imagining, or practicing? Or perhaps your son wants to play Catwoman or wishes to be the goddess Athena? If he learns that boys play male superheroes and gods, would he also shy away from imagining other roles for himself? Or what if he is a natural nurturer and wants to take in all the stray animals he finds? When you encourage a child to imagine, be aware of your own biases and the limitations of your own imagination. Whether the role is traditional or challenging the status quo, be the facilitator, not the judge, of your child's imagination.

Explore unconditionally. If we are to keep the world and all its opportunities open for children to explore, they must be encouraged to run with any ideas passing through their minds, unconditionally supported by their caregivers. If possible, take your child to museums, markets, festivals, art shows, and plays to encourage a broad creative perspective of the world. Another great thing to do is to simply ask your children, "Okay, who do you want to be?" or "In what land do you want to play?" and encourage whatever character or domain they create.

Monitor media consumption. The average child is overwhelmed with a deluge of passive learning from media—such as TV, the internet, and videogames—with little opportunity to create their worlds and identities through imagination and creativity. The issue is not only that passive "screen time" does not encourage imagination or participation on the part of the child, but also that the characters, images, and stories are often developmentally inappropriate for children and can shape their gender identities before they can even identify their gender. As a parent, you can ask open-ended questions to encourage your child to consider the possibilities for all genders. For example, you may say something like, "Why do you think all the superheroes on this show are boys? Couldn't a girl do the same thing?" The idea is not to give your child the answer, but to ask the questions to promote possibilities for her to imagine.

As we previously noted, the first female NFL referee had to believe in her potential without an existing role model to support her dream. We do not know what your child is going to become, but anything she can believe and create in her mind would be a good start. In therapy, we do not make people "better," as much as we help guide people to trust their visions of life and remove the barriers of doubt and fear that hold them back from their true potential. Our hope is that this book can serve as a step towards your child realizing his or her true potential.

About the Authors

Jeffrey Bone, PsyD, and Lisa Bone, PhD, are psychologists in private practice in Orange County, California. Jeffrey graduated from Kenyon College and the California School of Professional Psychology. Lisa graduated from the University of Alabama and the California School of Professional Psychology. They are parents to two girls, who have inspired them to create poetry and whimsical stories for their nightly entertainment. Their children are cute, but ferocious, and the authors do not dare to hold back silly words or ideas that make them laugh.

About the Illustrator

Valeria Docampo's inspiration for her art is rooted in everyday life: the eyes of a dog, the shape of a tree, the sound of rainfall, and the aromas of breakfast. Born in Buenos Aires, Argentina, she studied graphic design and visual communication at the University of Buenos Aires. She has illustrated several books for children, notably *Pequenos y Gigantes, Celebra Kwanzaa con Botitas y sus gatitos, La soupe à la tortue,* and *Phileas's Fortune,* a Magination Press book.

About Magination Press

Magination Press is an imprint of the American Psychological Association, the largest scientific and professional organization representing psychologists in the United States and the largest association of psychologists worldwide.